The Boxcar Children Mysteries

THE GIANT YO-YO
MYSTERY

created by
GERTRUDE CHANDLER WARNER

Illustrated by Robert Papp

ALBERT WHITMAN & Company
Morton Grove, IL

The Giant Yo-Yo Mystery
created by Gertrude Chandler Warner;
illustrated by Robert Papp.

ISBN 13 978-0-8075-0878-7 (hardcover)
ISBN 13 978-0-8075-0879-4 (paperback)

Cover art by Robert Papp.

For more information about Albert Whitman & Company,
visit our web site at www.albertwhitman.com.

Contents

THE GIANT YO-YO
MYSTERY

CHAPTER 1

An Unhappy Neighbor

"Hey, everyone!" six-year-old Benny Alden cried as he ran into the living room dragging an old red yo-yo by its string. "You'll never guess what I just did!"

Benny's ten-year-old sister, Violet, glanced up from her book. "What did you do, Benny?"

"Yes, tell us," twelve-year-old Jessie said eagerly. She and fourteen-year-old Henry were in the middle of a game of checkers.

Their grandfather, James Alden, set his newspaper aside. "Whatever it is must be

1

pretty exciting. You're all out of breath, Benny."

Benny grinned. "I know," he said, panting. "And my news is exciting." He took a deep breath, then said, "I just broke my own record!"

"Record for what?" Henry asked.

"Yo-yoing!" Benny held up his yo-yo. "My old record was 42. But I just made this yo-yo go down and up 57 times!"

"That's wonderful, Benny," Jessie said.

"It sure is," Grandfather agreed. He looked closer at the yo-yo in Benny's hand. "Hey, where did you get that yo-yo?"

"I found it out in the boxcar," Benny replied.

Back before the children had come to live with their grandfather, they lived in an old boxcar. Their parents had died and they didn't know their grandfather. They were afraid he'd be mean, so they ran away. They found an old boxcar in the woods and decided to live there.

When their grandfather found them, the children discovered he wasn't mean at all.

He brought them to live with him. He even had their boxcar moved to his backyard so they could play there anytime they wanted to.

Grandfather picked up the yo-yo and turned it around in his hand. The initials *J.A.* were carved into one side of the yo-yo.

"This looks like my old yo-yo," Grandfather said with a smile. "I thought this was in a box of old toys in the basement. I wonder how it got out to the boxcar?"

Benny looked the yo-yo over. "I bet I know," he said after a little while. He pointed to some tiny gouges in the wood. "See the teeth marks? I think Watch found it in the basement and took it outside."

The Aldens' dog slapped his tail on the floor and let out a friendly woof when he heard his name.

"I'll bet you're right," Henry said.

"Good detective work, Benny," Jessie said, scratching Watch behind the ears.

The Aldens were known for their detective skills. They had solved many mysteries since coming to live with their grandfather.

"Well, I'm glad you found it," Grandfather said, turning the yo-yo around in his hand. "I used to be quite good at this when I was a boy. I knew several tricks."

"Can you show us?" Violet asked.

"I don't know if I can still do this," Grandfather said. "Let's see . . ." He brought his hand up to his shoulder, flicked his wrist and sent the yo-yo down to the floor. It rolled along the carpet for a few feet, then Grandfather rolled it back up again.

"Wow!" Benny said, clapping his hands. "What's that trick called?"

"It's called 'walk the dog,'" Grandfather said.

"Can you show me how to do it?" Benny asked.

"Sure," Grandfather said. "First you have to learn to make the yo-yo 'sleep.'"

"Sleep?" Benny wrinkled his nose. "I thought only people and animals could go to sleep."

Grandfather chuckled. "Yo-yos can sleep, too. When a yo-yo sleeps, that just means it's spinning at the bottom of the string. Like this." Grandfather brought his hand up to his shoulder once again and sent the yo-yo down. The yo-yo stayed at the bottom of the string and spun around and around. It didn't come back up until Grandfather turned his hand around and pulled it back up.

"How did you do that?" Benny asked, wide-eyed.

"Let me show you," Grandfather said. He handed the yo-yo back to Benny. "Now, raise your arm up like you're lifting a weight. Then throw your arm forward and drop the yo-yo."

Benny tried to do what Grandfather said, but the yo-yo just wobbled at the bottom of the string and came to a stop. It didn't spin at all.

"It takes practice," Grandfather said. "If you learn how to throw a sleeper, then I'll show you how to walk the dog."

Benny nodded. "I'll keep working on it."

"What other tricks do you know, Grandfather?" Jessie asked.

"Oh, I used to do the 'rattlesnake,' 'man on the flying trapeze,' 'double or nothing,' 'the pinwheel' . . ." Grandfather smiled as he remembered. "But I'm not sure I can do any of those tricks anymore. Say, if you kids are interested in yo-yos, I should introduce you to my friend, Jeff Naylor. He's a furniture builder, but he knows some really fancy yo-yo tricks. In fact, he's in the middle of a new project that I think you kids would find interesting."

"What kind of project?" Henry asked.

"Jeff is trying to build the world's largest yo-yo," Grandfather explained. "It's pretty incredible. I saw it when I was in his shop just the other day."

"How big is the world's largest yo-yo?" Benny asked.

"I'm not sure," Grandfather said. "But I know that when Jeff's yo-yo is done, it's going to be so big that it'll be launched from a big crane."

"You mean it's actually going to go up and down like a regular yo-yo?" Jessie asked.

"That's what Jeff says," Grandfather replied.

"Can we see it go up and down?" Benny asked.

"I'm sure we can," Grandfather said. "Jeff says the whole town will be invited. Would you like me to take you to meet Jeff right now?"

"Oh yes," the children said eagerly.

The Aldens hopped into the car and Grandfather drove across town. Jeff's shop was in an over-sized, white building that sat on a corner of a residential street. It had a huge garage door in the front. The door looked big enough to drive a semi truck though. Beside it was a regular door. A sign in the small parking lot read: *Jeff's Custom Furniture*.

The children followed Grandfather across the parking lot. They could hear hammering, sawing, and loud music coming from inside the building.

Grandfather pushed open the door and the Aldens walked inside. The hammering, sawing, and music were so loud that Benny put his hands over his ears.

The inside of the building was one large open space. There were several unfinished wood cabinets scattered in the middle of the room, and a video camera sat on a tripod in the back corner.

A woman dressed in faded overalls was sawing boards at one end of the shop. Her brown, curly hair was tied back in a ponytail. She didn't notice the Aldens at first.

The man who was hammering boards together at the other end of the shop saw them walk in. He reached behind him and turned down the volume on the radio.

"James!" he exclaimed. "I'm so glad you stopped back. These must be your grandchildren."

"Yes. This is Henry, Jessie, Violet, and Benny." Grandfather introduced them. "Kids, this is my good friend, Jeff Naylor."

Jeff was a tall, thin man with very short hair and a nice smile. He shook hands with each of the children. "It's nice to meet you all."

Jeff cupped his hands around his mouth

and called, "Emily!" to the woman in overalls. He motioned for her to stop sawing for a minute.

Emily turned off the saw. "Yes?" she said loudly.

"I want to introduce you to some friends of mine," Jeff said. "These are the Aldens. Everyone, this is my assistant, Emily Kaye."

"Pleased to meet you," Emily said politely. Then she turned the saw back on and got right back to work.

"Emily is amazing," Jeff said loudly, leading the Aldens away from the noise. "I just hired her a couple months ago, but she jumped right in on this order of cabinets I have. I hardly had to train her. And then besides working hard for me all day, she's been staying after hours to help me with this yo-yo project."

"That's wonderful," Grandfather said. "I know you've had a hard time finding another carpenter after your old friend Gary Richmond quit."

A cloud passed in front of Jeff's eyes. "Gary Richmond is no friend of mine. And

I don't want to talk about him." He turned to the children. "Did you kids know I'm trying to build the world's largest yo-yo?"

"Yes. Grandfather told us," Jessie said in a loud voice so she could be heard over the saw.

"Is this it?" Benny asked as he gazed at the huge, round, wooden object behind Jeff. It was more than twice as wide across as Benny was tall. But it didn't look much like a yo-yo. It looked more like a huge bicycle wheel with spokes.

"Yes, this is it," Jeff said proudly. "Half of it, anyway. I have to build each half separately, then connect them with an axle."

"How big is it going to be when it's finished?" Jessie asked.

"Well, each of these halves will have a diameter of twelve feet," Jeff said.

"Twelve feet?" Benny cried, his eyes wide as golf balls. "That's as tall as the deep end of the swimming pool!"

"That's right." Jeff smiled. "And when the yo-yo is put together, it'll probably be about five feet wide and will weigh more than a thousand pounds."

"That's incredible," Henry said. "And it'll really go up and down, too?"

"Do you mean 'will it yo?'" Jeff asked. "That's what we say when a yo-yo goes up and down. And to answer your question, Henry, yes, when it's done this yo-yo should yo. It won't break the previous record if it doesn't."

"How can something so big . . . *yo?*" Jessie asked, trying out the new word. "Won't it be too heavy?"

"I'll have to use an extra strong cable for the string. And I'm planning to launch it from a two-hundred-foot crane. It should be fine—if I build it right. I've been working on this design for a couple of years. I've talked with engineers, geometry teachers, and physics teachers over at the community college. There's a lot of math involved in a project like this."

"I'm sure there is," Grandfather said.

"Would you like to see my drawings?" Jeff asked.

"Sure," the children said.

Jeff led everyone over to a pair of desks in the corner. One had a computer and printer on it. The other was a regular desk with drawers. Jeff opened the top drawer and pulled out some papers. But before he could explain what the papers were, the front door burst open and a very angry-looking older woman barged in.

"Mr. Naylor," the woman said through gritted teeth. "I know you run a business here, but it's after hours. Surely, you don't really need to be sawing now! Greenfield does have a city noise ordinance, you know."

Jeff motioned for Emily to stop sawing again. With a heavy sigh, Emily shut off the saw.

"I'm sorry about the noise, Mrs. Thorton," Jeff said. "We didn't mean to disturb you. But this project isn't anything I've been hired to do, so I didn't feel right working on it during business hours."

Mrs. Thorton's eyes narrowed. "What exactly are you doing?" she asked.

"He's building the world's largest yo-yo!" Benny said.

"Really?" Mrs. Thorton said.

"Yes." Jeff spread out his papers on top of the desk and started to explain how the yo-yo would work.

But Mrs. Thorton interrupted him. "I don't like the sound of this, Jeff. It sounds dangerous."

"I assure you, Mrs. Thorton, I am taking every possible safety precaution."

"But you're talking about launching a thousand-pound yo-yo from two hundred feet in the air! How can that possibly be safe?"

"Well—" Jeff began.

"No!" Mrs. Thorton shook her head. "I'm asking you as a good neighbor, Jeff. Please don't do this."

Jeff took a deep breath. "I'm sorry, Mrs. Thorton. I can try and do something about the noise, but I can't give up this project. Karl's Lumber is donating wood. A-1 Wrecking is donating use of the crane. People are excited about this project. If the yo-yo works, it'll put Greenfield on the map!"

"But what if that yo-yo falls from

the crane and rolls into the crowd?" Mrs. Thorton asked. "Someone could get hurt. Maybe even killed."

Jeff opened his mouth to protest, but Mrs. Thorton cut him off. "I'm warning you, Jeff, if you don't stop this project, I'll find a way to stop you."

And with that, Mrs. Thorton stormed out of the shop.

CHAPTER 2

Mystery Vehicle

"Who was that lady?" Benny asked. "She didn't seem very friendly."

"That's Mrs. Thorton," Jeff replied. "She lives in that little yellow house across the street. And it's not that she's unfriendly. She just worries a lot."

"What does she worry about?" Violet asked.

"You name it, Mrs. Thorton worries about it," Emily muttered as she carried an armload of wood pieces over to where Jeff had been assembling the yo-yo.

"But why is she so worried about the yo-yo?" Benny asked. "Could it really fall from the crane and roll into the crowd and hurt people?"

Jeff got down on his knees so he was at eye-level with Benny. "I promise you, Benny, I won't put the yo-yo up on the crane if I'm not one-hundred-percent sure it's safe. I don't want people to get hurt any more than you or Mrs. Thorton do."

"I'm sure Jeff knows what he's doing, Benny," Grandfather said.

"That's right," Emily said. "He's been poring over those plans for months. He probably knows more about building huge yo-yos than he does about building furniture."

Jeff laughed. "That's probably true."

"Do you think Mrs. Thorton will really try and stop you from building the yo-yo?" Jessie asked.

"She might try," Jeff said. "She'll probably talk to the mayor. I know the two of them are good friends. But I don't think she'll have any luck stopping the project. The only reason she might have to complain would be noise. And I'm going to see what I can do about that."

"Could you do the noisy work earlier in the day?" Violet suggested.

"That's exactly what I was thinking," Jeff said. "I've been doing my regular work during the day and saving the yo-yo for after hours. But lately, my regular work has been staining cabinets. Staining cabinets doesn't make any noise. I could do that just as easily at night."

"Mrs. Thorton isn't even home until late afternoon," Emily said. "We could do the sawing for the yo-yo during the day while she's gone. As long as we meet the deadline on these cabinets, it probably doesn't matter what we do when, does it?"

"I don't think so," Jeff said. "It's settled then. Starting tomorrow, we'll do the yo-yo work during the day and the cabinet work at night."

Honk! Honk! A horn blared outside.

Emily turned toward the door. "Oh, that's probably Todd," she said. She took off her safety goggles and hung them on a hook in the corner. Then she grabbed her purse and sweater.

"It was nice meeting you," Emily told the Aldens. "I'll see you tomorrow, Jeff." She waved, then hurried out the door just as the car outside honked again.

Jeff shook his head. "That Emily is a nice girl, but I don't think much of her boyfriend, Todd. Every night it's the same. He comes to pick her up, but instead of coming inside to see if she's ready, he just sits out front and honks until she comes out."

"That's not very polite," Violet said.

"No, it isn't," Jeff agreed. "I know he doesn't like her working late, so I wonder what he's going to say when we start working on the yo-yo during the day and then doing our other work at night? She won't be able to leave when he honks then. But I guess it's not my place to worry about it."

Jeff turned back to the papers on his desk. "I just hope I don't have any trouble with Mrs. Thorton. I've always had a passion for yo-yos, and I would really like to build the world's largest yo-yo."

"We hope you don't have any trouble with her, either," Violet said.

Jeff smiled. "Say, did you kids know that the word *yo-yo* means 'come come?'"

"No," the children all said at once.

"It's true," Jeff said. "It comes from a Tagalog word. Tagalog is a language that's spoken in the Philippines."

"Is that where the yo-yo was invented?" Violet asked.

"No, I think the yo-yo was invented in China," Jeff said. "It was certainly used in the Philippines, though. In fact, at one time it was used as a hunting weapon. Hunters would throw it out to try and catch an animal by the legs."

"Really?" Henry said. "That's interesting."

"Yes. The yo-yo has a pretty interesting history," Jeff said. "I've got some articles here if you'd like to read more about it."

"I'd like to," Violet said. "I'll bring them back as soon as I've finished reading them."

"Take your time," Jeff said. "You know, I sure could use some more help with this yo-yo. What do you kids say? Would you like to help build the world's largest yo-yo?"

"Oh boy!" Benny cried. "Could we, Grandfather?"

"I don't know why not," Grandfather said.

"What would you want us to do?" Jessie asked.

"Nothing too hard," Jeff said. "Looks like Emily has mostly finished cutting the pieces for the first half of the yo-yo, so until I get another delivery of wood, it's just a matter of screwing the pieces together. Eventually, I'll need help getting the two halves connected to the axle and then we'll need to paint the outside."

"We can help with all of that!" Violet said eagerly.

"I'll also need someone to run the video camera every now and then." Jeff pointed to the camera that was sitting on a tripod in the corner.

"Are you making a movie about building the yo-yo?" Grandfather asked.

"Sort of," Jeff said. "If you want to break a world's record, you need to document every step along the way so that people know you really did it."

"I know how to run a video camera," Benny said, jumping up and down.

"That's good, Benny," Jeff said with a smile. "It sounds like you're all good helpers. Do you think you could come back tomorrow morning?"

"We'd love to!" The children nodded eagerly.

"In that case, we'd better get home and get you all to bed," Grandfather said.

"Okay," the children agreed. They all said their goodbyes, then the Aldens headed out to the car.

Grandfather's car was parked on the street, right in front of a gray station wagon. It looked like there was somebody inside the station wagon wearing a dark baseball cap. It was too dark to tell whether the person was a man or a woman, but Henry wondered why the person was just sitting there.

Henry reached for the handle on Grandfather's car when suddenly Jeff came out of the shop. "Wait, James! Children!" Jeff yelled as he hurried toward them waving some rolled-up papers.

"What is it, Jeff?" Grandfather called from the car.

Jeff handed Henry the papers. "I wanted you to take these plans for the yo-yo home tonight so you can look them over and see how everything fits together."

"We'd like that," Henry said as he slipped the plans inside his green backpack, then zipped it up. "Thank you."

"Terrific," Jeff said. "I'll see you all tomorrow."

The Aldens chatted about how much fun they were going to have building the world's largest yo-yo as they piled into the car. Grandfather pulled out into the street. As he did, Henry noticed the lights on the vehicle behind them come on.

Henry turned around in his seat. The station wagon was pulling out right behind them. At first, Henry wasn't too concerned.

After all, it could be a coincidence that

the person in the station wagon happened to be leaving the same time the Aldens were.

But then Grandfather turned right at the next intersection. He drove three blocks, then turned left. Henry turned around again. The station wagon was two vehicles behind them.

Jessie peered curiously at Henry. "What's the matter, Henry?" she asked.

"I don't know," Henry said, watching the station wagon curiously. "I think we're being followed."

"Followed?" Grandfather asked. He glanced in his rearview mirror. Jessie, Violet, and Benny turned around, too.

"Who's following us?" Benny wanted to know.

"Not the vehicle right behind us," Henry said. "It's the one behind that. The gray station wagon. I noticed it parked behind us at Jeff's. Then, when we pulled out, so did that car. It's been behind us ever since we left."

"Why would someone want to follow us?" Violet asked.

"I don't know," Henry said.

Grandfather made another right turn, and everyone watched anxiously to see what the station wagon would do. It made a right turn, too.

"Hmm," Grandfather said. He turned right again at the next intersection and the Aldens found themselves on a well-lit street with lots of stores.

"I wonder what our friend back there will do if we pull over?" Grandfather mused. He signaled, then pulled off to the side of the road.

Everyone watched the station wagon.

It kept right on going until it was out of sight.

"Did anyone get a good look at the driver?" Grandfather asked.

"No," Violet said. "It was too dark."

"And they went by too fast," Benny said.

"It's possible we weren't even being followed at all," Henry said.

"It's possible," Jessie agreed. "But I think we should keep an eye out for that vehicle. See if we notice it again."

Violet nodded in agreement. "Maybe we can ask Jeff tomorrow whether he knows of anyone in the neighborhood who drives a car like that."

"Good thinking," Henry said.

"At any rate, we're not being followed now," Grandfather said. He waited for an opening in the traffic, then pulled out into the street and headed for home.

CHAPTER 3

Trouble in the Shop

Grandfather drove the children back to Jeff's shop early the next morning. He couldn't pull into the parking lot because Emily was standing there with a man dressed in black jeans and a black jacket. So Grandfather pulled up along the side of the road to let the children out.

As Benny got out of the car, he noticed Mrs. Thorton standing in the front window of her little yellow house across the street.

"Hey, there's that lady who came into Jeff's shop last night," Benny said. He raised his hand to wave at her, but as soon as he did, Mrs. Thorton pulled her curtains closed.

"I thought Emily said she wasn't home much during the day," Jessie said.

"It looks like she's home today," Violet said.

"Why don't you kids call me when you're ready to come home," Grandfather said.

"We will," Henry promised as he hoisted his backpack up onto his back.

Grandfather drove away as the children walked over to the shop.

Emily and the man in black were still deep in conversation. They didn't notice the children.

"Trust me," Emily said. "I'm taking care of it. We won't have to worry about that silly yo-yo much longer."

The children stopped and stared. What did Emily mean by that?

"I hope you're right," the man in black said. He squeezed Emily's hand, then walked down the sidewalk.

Emily turned to go inside. But when she

saw the Aldens, she jumped.

"What are you kids doing here?" She scowled at them.

"We were just going inside," Violet said. "Jeff asked us to come down here this morning to help with the yo-yo."

Emily pressed her lips together, then said, "Well, it's not nice to eavesdrop on other people's conversations. You could misinterpret what you hear."

"We know that," Henry said. "And we weren't eavesdropping. Honest."

Henry wanted to ask Emily what she'd meant by "I'm taking care of it. We won't have to worry about that silly yo-yo anymore." But Emily already seemed angry; he didn't want to make her any angrier. So he and his brother and sisters followed Emily into the shop.

When they got inside, they found Jeff pacing around the workshop, talking on his cell phone. He looked irritated.

"I don't understand," Jeff said into his phone. "Where would you get the idea I didn't want that order of wood? Uh huh . . . A woman, huh?" He glanced over at Emily, who was hanging up her jacket and not paying any attention to Jeff's conversation. "I'll see what I can find out on this end and get back to you. I do want the wood, though, Karl. I want it as soon as you can get it to me."

Jeff slapped his cell phone closed and nodded at the children. "I'll be with you kids in a minute," he said. He strode over to Emily. "Did you cancel that next order of wood?"

"I—" Emily began, her face turning red. She didn't finish her sentence. But it was clear she had canceled the wood.

Jeff let out a breath of air. "Why in the world would you do that?"

"I-I didn't think we needed any more wood." She pointed to the yo-yo piece that Jeff had been working on. "It looks like we're almost done. So when Karl called yesterday, I told him we didn't need that other order."

"We're almost done with the one half of the yo-yo," Jeff said. "We still have a whole other half to build."

"Oh. I didn't realize," Emily said. "I'm so sorry."

The Aldens exchanged looks. It seemed strange that someone who knew as much about woodworking as Emily would forget about the second half of the yo-yo.

Jeff softened. "Well, it was an honest mistake. And there's nothing we can do about it now. Karl will get a new load of wood over here as soon as he can. It just won't be today. In the meantime, Emily, why don't you work on those cabinets. The Aldens can help me with the boards that we have."

"Okay," Emily said.

"Benny, would you like to run the video camera for me?" Jeff asked.

"Sure," Benny said, skipping over to the camera.

"I'm just going to get some safety goggles for all of us," Jeff said. He pulled a bunch of safety goggles out of a box and started handing them around.

"Hey, there's something wrong with this

camera," Benny spoke up. "It won't turn on."

Jessie went over to help Benny. She pushed a button, then said, "Well, no wonder it won't turn on. There's no flash card in here."

"No flash card?" Jeff frowned. He strode over to the camera and checked for himself. "You're right, Benny. I don't understand. I haven't taken the flash card out of this camera. I've been recording on it for the last week."

Jeff walked over to Emily. "Did you take the flash card out of the video camera?"

Emily glanced up from the cabinet she was staining. "Why would I do that?" she asked.

"Do you have another flash card?" Violet asked.

"Yes." Jeff walked over to his desk, opened the top drawer and pulled out another flash card. "But I need to find out what happened to the first card. I recorded everything I've done on the yo-yo up to now on there. Without it, I won't get credit for the record."

"Did you copy what was on the other card to your computer?" Henry asked.

Jeff shook his head. "Unfortunately, no. I figured I'd do that once I filled the card."

"I hope you find it," Violet said as Jeff inserted the new flash card into the camera.

"I'm sure it's around," Jeff said.

Then they all got to work screwing boards together. Jeff's plans showed exactly where each piece was supposed to go. The Aldens checked the plans every time they added a new board.

"Hmm," Henry said, squinting at the plans. "Am I really supposed to put another piece here? The drawing shows another piece, but there's a note here that says to wait on that piece."

Jessie and Violet gathered around Henry and studied the plans over his shoulder. There were a lot of extra directions written on the margins of the paper. The directions were written in red pen with a different handwriting.

"Who made all these red notes?" Jessie

asked Jeff. "Are we supposed to do what the notes say or follow the original plans?"

Jeff peered at the plans. "Just follow the original plan," he said stiffly. "Those red notes were made by my former partner, Gary Richmond."

"Were you and Gary going to build this yo-yo together?" Violet asked.

Jeff sighed. "At one time, yes. Gary and I always talked about breaking a world's record together. Ever since we were kids. First we were going to build the world's tallest house of cards. We were both good at building houses of cards, but not that good.

"Then we decided we were going to make the world's largest pizza. But we couldn't figure out how to bake it. A few years ago we decided we should go for a record that involved woodworking, since we both know something about that. So we started making plans to build the world's largest yo-yo."

"Why isn't Gary working on the yo-yo with you now?" Violet asked.

"We had a falling out a few months ago," Jeff said sadly. "We're not friends anymore."

"Can't you just be friends again?" Benny asked.

"I thought so at first," Jeff said. "That's why I held off on building the yo-yo for a little while. But the more time that went by, the clearer it became that Gary and I would never be friends again. I knew that if I still wanted to build the yo-yo, I would have to do it without him."

"What happened between the two of you?" Jessie asked.

Jeff sighed. "It's a long story. But basically, we had a difference of opinion on where to take the business. He wanted to grow the business and bring in new employees. I prefer to stay small. This difference of opinion grew and grew until it finally broke up our friendship."

"I'm sorry to hear that," Violet said.

"Me too," Jeff said.

"Does Gary know you're building this yo-yo?" Henry asked.

"I don't think so," Jeff said. "We haven't

spoken in months. Look, I don't want to talk about this anymore. If you have questions about the plans, just follow the original instructions. I don't feel right using Gary's notes when he's not involved in the project anymore."

With that, Jeff strolled over to the door and stared outside.

"What a sad story about Jeff and his friend," Violet said. "I wish there was something we could do to help."

"Maybe if we think about it for a while, we'll come up with something." Henry said.

"Maybe," Jessie agreed.

The children got back to work. They screwed together all the boards that were left. When they finished, the first half of the yo-yo was almost complete.

"You kids did a great job," Jeff said.

"Thanks," Jessie said. "It was fun."

Benny stopped the camera. "Do you want to back up what's on the flash card, Jeff?"

"Since I seem to have lost my other flash card, yes, I think that would be a good idea," Jeff replied.

Benny took the flash card out of the camera and handed it to Jeff.

"Thanks, Benny," Jeff said. He rubbed his chin. "I sure wish I knew what happened to that other card. I've looked all over my desk for it. I just don't know where it could be."

"It'll turn up," Jessie said confidently.

"Hey, Jeff," Benny said, reaching into his pocket. "Grandfather said you know a lot of yo-yo tricks. Can you show us one before we leave?" He handed Jeff his yo-yo.

Jeff smiled. "What kind of trick would you like to see?"

"What's the hardest trick you know?" Benny asked.

"Hmm. The hardest trick I know . . . " Jeff had to think about it for a few seconds. "That would probably be the atom smasher."

"Can you show us?" Jessie asked.

"Sure." Jeff said. He dribbled Benny's yo-yo up and down a couple times to get a feel for it. Then he threw a fast sleeper, picked up the string in a couple of places, and the yo-yo first flipped onto one string, then did a somersault, ran down another string, did another somersault and finally landed back in Jeff's hand.

The whole thing happened so fast, the Aldens weren't entirely sure what exactly they'd seen. But it sure was impressive.

"That was really neat," Violet said.

"Thank you," Jeff replied.

"I'm still trying to learn how to do a sleeper," Benny said. "I haven't been able to do it yet."

"You keep working on it, Benny," Jeff said. "You'll get it."

"Well, we don't want to keep you from your work, Jeff," Henry said. "When would you like us to come back again?"

"There's not much more we can do until I get some more wood. How about I call you when I've got more for you to do?"

"Okay," Violet said.

Jeff walked the children to the door. As soon as they stepped outside, they noticed the gray station wagon was back. It was parked in front of Mrs. Thorton's house.

But this time it didn't look like there was anyone inside.

"Hey, Jeff," Henry said. "Have you ever seen that gray station wagon before?"

Jeff glanced over to where Henry was pointing. "Can't say that I have," he said. "Why do you ask?"

"It was parked behind our grandfather's car last night," Jessie explained. "In fact, when we left, it left, too. For a while we thought whoever was driving that car was following us. But then Grandfather pulled over and the person kept right on going."

"Well, I can't imagine why anyone would want to follow you," Jeff said. "And I don't know whose vehicle it is, unless it belongs to Mrs. Thorton's son. I think I heard he was in town this week."

"That's probably whose it is," Violet said. That would also explain why Mrs. Thorton was home during the day today.

"So it's probably a coincidence that he happened to leave the same time we did last night," Henry said.

"I don't know Erik Thorton," Jeff said.

"But rumor has it he set out to break a world's record a few years ago, too."

"Really?" Benny asked. "Which record?"

"I can't remember," Jeff said, scratching his head. "I don't even remember whether he was successful. But I know there were articles about it in the newspaper. You could probably find them if you were really interested."

"Hey, Jeff?" Emily called. "Could you come help me move this cabinet?"

"Sure," Jeff said. He hurried over to her.

The Aldens were about to leave when the phone next to Jessie rang.

"Could one of you get that?" Jeff called to the Aldens. He had one end of a heavy cabinet and Emily had the other. They were maneuvering it over to the back of the shop. "I'll be there in a minute."

"Sure," Jessie said, picked up the phone. "Jeff's Custom Furniture."

A male voice said, "Tell Jeff to stop building that yo-yo!"

Jessie frowned. "Excuse me?"

"You heard me," the voice said. "I'm

warning you, if Jeff doesn't stop, there will be trouble."

"Who is this?" Jessie asked. "Hello? Hello?"

But whoever it was had already hung up.

"Who is it?" Jeff asked as he walked across the shop.

Jessie hung up the phone. "I don't know. He didn't give a name. He said, 'Tell Jeff to stop building that yo-yo.' And then he said, 'I'm warning you, if Jeff doesn't stop, there will be trouble.'"

Violet looked alarmed. "What kind of trouble?"

"I don't know," Jessie said. "That's all he said."

"Well, I don't respond to threats," Jeff said. "I'm not quitting this project just because someone calls up and tells me there will be trouble if I don't."

"Good," Henry said. He didn't want Jeff to stop building the yo-yo, but still, the phone call made him a little nervous.

CHAPTER 4

A Trip to the Library

"I wonder who made that phone call," Jessie said a few minutes later. The Aldens were gathered in the small parking lot outside Jeff's shop.

"I don't know," Henry said, hoisting his backpack onto his shoulder. "But I don't like it."

While they were standing there, Benny noticed a curtain moving in the front window of the little yellow house across the street. Was Mrs. Thorton watching them again? He wondered.

"Remember, Mrs. Thorton said she'd do whatever it took to stop Jeff from building the yo-yo?" Benny asked.

"Yes," the others said.

"Maybe she's the one who made the phone call," Benny suggested.

"I don't think so," Jessie said. "The voice on the phone was definitely a man's voice."

"Then maybe it was her son," Benny said. "Jeff also said he thought her son Erik was visiting right now."

"Why would he call Jeff?" Henry asked. "Just because his mother thinks the yo-yo is too dangerous?"

"I don't know. That doesn't make a lot of sense," Jessie said.

"I wonder what record Erik Thorton tried to break." Violet said.

"Maybe we should go over to the library and see if we can find out?" Jessie suggested.

Jeff's shop was only a few blocks from the library, so Henry opened his backpack and took out his cell phone. Then he called Grandfather to see if it was okay if he,

Jessie, Violet, and Benny went to the library before Grandfather picked them up. Maybe they could even have lunch at the Greenfield Diner along the way.

"That sounds like a nice idea," Grandfather said. "Call me when you're finished at the library."

So the children headed downtown. The diner was on the corner of Center Street and 4th Avenue. Bells jangled on the door when the Aldens stepped inside.

"Have a seat anywhere," a waitress called as she delivered an armload of plates to the people in the back booth.

The Aldens chose a table near the front door, then opened their menus.

The waitress poured water for each of them, then took out her pad and pen. "What'll it be?" she asked, chomping on her gum.

The children all ordered cheeseburgers, fries, and vanilla milkshakes. Then they sat back to wait for their order.

"I want to get some books on yo-yos when we're at the library," Benny said.

"Maybe I can find one with pictures on how to do a sleeper."

"I'd like to get some books on yo-yos, too," Violet said. "Did you know that the yo-yo is the second oldest toy in history?"

"It is?" Jessie asked.

"Yes," Violet said. "Yo-yos have been around for twenty-five hundred years. I read that in one of those articles that Jeff gave me."

"If the yo-yo is the second oldest toy, I wonder what the oldest toy is?" Benny said.

"The doll," Violet said. "I read that in the same article. I'd like to see what else I can find out about the history of yo-yos."

The waitress brought their food and the children dug in.

"Mm!" Benny said as he wrapped his mouth around the huge burger. "I'm starving!"

"You're always starving, Benny," Violet teased. She took a sip of her milkshake. As she put her glass down, she noticed a gray station wagon parked across the street.

"I don't believe it!" Violet said, staring out the window.

"What?" Jessie asked. She turned around in her seat to see what Violet was looking at.

"That same gray station wagon we saw in front of Jeff's shop last night and this morning is now parked right out in front of this diner," Violet said.

"Is there anybody in it?" Henry asked, straining his neck to see.

"No," Violet replied. "Do you still think it's a coincidence we keep seeing that car?"

"I don't know," Henry said with concern. "The more often we see it, the more I wonder if we're being followed."

"But why would anyone want to follow us?" Jessie asked.

"I don't know," Violet said.

* * * *

"We're looking for some information on Erik Thorton," Jessie told the reference librarian.

"What kind of information are you looking for?" the librarian asked.

Henry let his backpack drop to the floor. "Well, we know he grew up here in Greenfield, but he doesn't live here anymore. We heard he tried to break a world's record a few years ago. We'd like to know what that record was."

"And whether he actually broke it or not," Benny put in.

"It sounds like you want some magazine or newspaper articles," the librarian said. She showed them how to search magazine and newspaper databases.

"If you find something, let me know," the librarian said. "I'll see if we have the actual magazine or newspaper that you're looking for."

The children set their jackets and Henry's backpack on a table, and decided to look on the Internet first. When there were no matches for Erik Thornton, they started to search the library indexes for newspaper or magazine articles.

"Here's one," Violet said, sitting up a

little straighter. "It's an article from the *Greenfield Gazette*. 'Local Boy Attempts World's Record.'"

"What's the record for?" Benny stood on his tip-toes, trying to see. "Does it say?"

"Oh, wow," Jessie said, staring at the computer screen. "You're not going to believe this."

"What?" Violet asked.

"It looks like Erik Thorton tried to build the world's largest yo-yo, too."

"No! Really?" Henry said.

"There's just one sentence that says what the article is about," Jessie said. "If we want to know more, we have to get the whole article."

"Are there other articles about him besides this one?" Violet asked.

Jessie scanned the listings on the computer screen. "It looks like there were several articles about him in the *Greenfield Gazette*."

Henry copied down the information. Then he said, "Let's go ask the librarian if they've got these newspapers here."

The children trooped back over to the reference desk.

"We do have that newspaper," the librarian told them. "But it's on microfiche. Do you know how to use the microfiche machine?"

"No," Jessie said. "But we're willing to learn."

The librarian took the children over to a cabinet and pulled out a small box with the correct date. "This roll contains the newspaper you want," she said. Then she led the children over to the microfiche machine, turned on the lamp, and showed them how to thread the machine.

A page from an old *Greenfield Gazette* came up on the screen.

"Cool!" Benny said.

"Now all you have to do is turn this handle to go forward," the librarian said, as she demonstrated. "This other handle goes backward. You just keep turning the handles until you get to the article you want."

Jessie turned the handle and pages flew by on the screen in front of them.

"What date are we looking for?" Violet asked.

"October 26," Jessie replied. Finally, she got to the right date. The article they were looking for was on page 4.

Jessie skimmed through the article. "This one just talks about him building the yo-yo. It doesn't say whether he actually finished it or whether it broke any records."

"It looks like his yo-yo was only eight feet tall," Henry said. "Jeff's yo-yo is going to be much bigger than that."

"If I were Erik Thorton, I wouldn't be very happy about someone else trying to break my record," Benny said.

"We don't even know for sure that he set a record," Violet pointed out.

"Maybe the next article will tell us that," Jessie said. She turned the crank again, searching for the next article.

"Here it is," Jessie said, peering at the screen.

"Oh no!" Violet gasped.

"What?" Benny asked. He was a good reader for his age, but there were a lot of hard words in these articles.

"It says here that they used a crane to lift the yo-yo up into the air," Henry began.

"That's what Jeff's going to do, too," Violet said.

"Yes, but it says here that when they raised Erik's yo-yo, the rope broke and the yo-yo fell," Henry said. "Some people got hurt, including Erik. He broke his arm."

"Oh no," Benny said.

"The record never made it into any record books," Violet said. "It never counted at all."

"No wonder Mrs. Thorton doesn't want Jeff to build the world's largest yo-yo," Jessie said. "It looks like this time she's got a reason to be worried."

"Do you suppose that's why Erik is in town right now?" Henry asked. "To put a stop to Jeff's yo-yo?"

"How would Erik have known Jeff was trying to build the world's largest yo-yo?" Violet asked.

"Maybe his mother told him," Benny suggested.

"He could be the person who called earlier and told me to tell Jeff to stop building the yo-yo," Jessie suggested.

"Could be," Henry said. "But that doesn't explain why he'd follow us around. What would he want with us?"

"We don't know for sure that he has a gray station wagon," Violet pointed out.

Jessie stood up. "Well, either way, I think we're done here, aren't we? Why don't we go pick up our things at the table. Then we can take the microfiche back to the librarian and call Grandfather to see if he's ready to pick us up."

"Sounds good," Henry said as he led the way back to the table.

He handed Jessie her jacket. Violet grabbed her jacket and Benny's. Henry found his own jacket on the floor. He picked it up, then glanced around.

"Hey, where's my backpack?" Henry asked.

"Did you leave it over by the microfiche machine?" Jessie asked.

"No." Henry shook his head. "I'm sure

I left it here with the jackets."

But the table was empty. And Henry's backpack was nowhere to be seen.

CHAPTER 5

Missing Plans

Jessie went back to the microfiche machine. She searched all around it, but Henry's backpack wasn't there.

Violet and Benny checked under all the tables and chairs while Henry paced nervously back and forth.

"My cell phone was in there," he moaned. "And so were our library books and the plans for Jeff's yo-yo."

Violet bit her lip.

"Any luck?" Jessie asked when she returned from the microfiche machine.

The others all shook their heads.

Jessie sighed. "Maybe someone picked it up by mistake?" she offered.

"We could see if the library has a lost and found," Violet suggested.

So the Aldens headed back to the reference desk. Jessie turned in the microfiche film they had borrowed. Then Henry said, "Do you have a lost and found here? My backpack seems to be missing."

"We do," the librarian said. "I don't think we have any backpacks in there right now, but I can go take a look. What does yours look like?"

"It's green on the top and black on the sides, and it's got two big pockets on the front," Henry said.

The librarian tapped her fingers on the counter. "You know, I saw a gentleman with a backpack like that just a few minutes ago. I saw him go into the men's room. I don't know if he's still in the library or if he left after that."

"Thanks," Jessie said to the librarian as they moved away from the desk. She turned to Henry. "Maybe you and Benny can check out the men's room and the first floor of the library while Violet and I search the second floor."

"Good idea," Henry said.

So the four of them split up. Jessie and Violet started walking up and down the fiction aisles, searching every shelf they passed. They'd gotten through five aisles when Benny came to get them.

"Henry found his backpack," Benny said. "It was in the men's room."

Jessie, Violet, and Benny went to meet Henry in the library lobby. They found him sitting on a bench, rifling through his backpack.

"Is everything there?" Violet asked worriedly.

"Everything except the plans for Jeff's yo-yo," Henry replied.

* * * *

"I hope Jeff has another copy of those plans," Violet said as the children left the library.

"I'm sure he does," Henry said. "I can't believe he'd give us his only copy. Still, it bothers me that we lost them. Jeff trusted us."

"We didn't just lose them," Jessie pointed out. "Somebody stole them. Somebody knew they were in your bag, Henry, and they took them out of there."

"Maybe it was the person who drives the gray station wagon." Henry said. "Maybe he saw Jeff give them to me last night and that's why he followed us."

"But he probably didn't want us to know he was following us last night," Benny said. "That's why he kept going when Grandfather pulled over."

"And that's why he's been more careful about staying out of sight today," Henry said. "We've seen the car, but we've never seen the person driving it."

"Jeff thinks the car belongs to Erik Thorton," Violet said as they crossed Second Street. "But why would Erik want the plans for the yo-yo? He wants Jeff to quit building the yo-yo because he and his mom are afraid the yo-yo will fall and people will get hurt, right?"

"That's probably what Mrs. Thorton is worried about," Jessie said. "But maybe Erik has other ideas."

"What do you mean, Jessie?" Benny asked.

"Well, maybe Erik still wants to build the world's largest yo-yo himself? Maybe he stole Jeff's plans to see if Jeff has a better idea of how to do it than he had?"

"That's an interesting theory, Jessie," Henry said.

"In fact, maybe he took the flash card out of Jeff's camera, too, so he could see how Jeff built the yo-yo so far," Benny added.

"Maybe we should go back to Jeff's shop and ask him whether Erik has ever been in the shop," Jessie said.

"That's a good idea," Henry said. "And I should tell Jeff that the yo-yo plans are missing."

So the children made one more call to Grandfather, then walked back to the shop.

"I don't see that gray station wagon,"

Violet said as they turned onto the street where Jeff's shop was. But there was a blue truck parked in the small lot in front of Jeff's shop.

"I wonder whose truck that is," Benny said.

The Aldens walked across the parking lot and went inside Jeff's shop.

Emily whirled around when the door opened. She was standing at the printer. Her boyfriend Todd was spinning in Jeff's chair.

"What are you kids doing here?" Todd asked, glaring at them.

"We came to talk to Jeff," Violet said.

"Well, Jeff isn't here," Emily said impatiently. She turned back to the printer and tugged at a piece of paper that seemed to be stuck inside.

"Do you know when he'll be back?" Henry asked. "Nope," Emily said. "You can wait around for him if you want. But I've got everything done that I can do today, so I'm heading out. As soon as I get this paper out." She tugged at the paper some more.

"Looks like you've got a paper jam there," Jessie said. "Maybe I can help?"

Emily stepped aside as Jessie walked over to the printer. Jessie tried pushing the clear jam button on the printer, but that didn't work. So she turned the printer around, opened the back panel and pulled out a crumpled sheet of paper.

"Here you go." Jessie started to hand the paper to Emily, but then she noticed what the first couple lines of the paper said. *Dear Jeff, I've really enjoyed working for you these last couple of months, but the time has come for me to move on.*

Jessie looked at Emily. "Are you quitting your job?" she asked.

Emily took the paper from Jessie. "Yes, I'm quitting. Todd is opening his own custom furniture shop. I'll work for Jeff for two more weeks. Then I'm going to work for Todd."

Emily wadded up the paper in her hand and tossed it in the garbage can. "I think I better reprint this," she said.

Todd sighed. He checked his watch. "Well, hurry up. We need to get going."

Emily went to the computer, opened her document and started it printing it again.

"Does Jeff know you're quitting?" Henry asked. Jeff seemed to really like Emily. He wasn't going to be happy to hear she was quitting.

"Not yet," Emily admitted. "But he'll find out tomorrow when he gets this letter. I'll talk to him about it then."

Todd stood up. "Are you ready to go, Emily?" Todd asked.

"Just about," Emily said. She stuck her safety goggles in the pocket of her work jacket, hung the jacket up, then she picked up her purse from the floor. There was a rolled-up paper sticking out of the purse. It looked like there were math formulas on the paper.

"Hey, what's that paper in your bag?" Benny asked. Was it the plans for the yo-yo?

"This?" Emily asked, pulling the rolled-up paper out and glancing at it.

"Oh, that's nothing," she said. She quickly shoved the paper all the way down the bag and turned to her boyfriend. "We should go."

"Yes," he said, his hand on the doorknob. "See you kids later."

"Make sure you lock up when you leave," Emily told the children. "We wouldn't want anyone to break into Jeff's shop during the night."

Then Emily and Todd were gone.

CHAPTER 6

Sabotage

"Did you all see that paper that was sticking up out of Emily's bag?" Benny asked.

"I noticed it when you asked her about it, Benny," Violet said. "It looked like it had a yo-yo on it. And some math formulas."

"I saw that, too," Henry said.

"You don't think Emily could have followed us downtown and then taken them out of Henry's backpack, do you?" Jessie asked.

"I don't know," Benny said. "She was

here when we got here."

"Yes, but whoever took the plans out of Henry's backpack left the library before we did," Violet said. "He, or she, could've gotten back here ahead of us—especially if the person was driving. Driving is faster than walking."

"But Emily doesn't drive a gray station wagon," Henry said.

"We don't know what she drives," Jessie said. "She always leaves the shop with her boyfriend."

"Maybe her boyfriend drives a gray station wagon." Benny said.

"There was a blue truck parked out front when we got here. I'm guessing that's Emily's boyfriend's truck," Violet said.

"Could be," Jessie said. "Or it could be Emily's truck."

"Well, the person who picked up my backpack in the library was a man," Henry said.

"And the person who called here and told Jeff to stop building the yo-yo was also a man," Jessie said.

"But despite what Emily said, those sure looked like plans for the yo-yo in her bag," Benny said. "So if she didn't steal them out of Henry's backpack, I'd like to know where she got them."

"Or why she would want them," added Violet. "Emily could have taken the plans from the shop at any time."

Jessie sat down at Jeff's computer and looked at the screen. Emily had never closed the file with her resignation letter.

"I can't imagine why Emily would want the plans for the yo-yo," Jessie said as she closed the file on the computer. "She's quitting her job."

"Maybe Todd wants them for some reason." Henry said.

"Why would he want them?" Benny asked.

"I don't know," Henry said. "Maybe he wants to build the world's largest yo-yo, too, but he doesn't know how to do it."

Violet sighed. "It seems like we have more questions than we have answers."

The children waited a little longer for

Jeff to come back, but after awhile, they decided to leave, too. They called Grandfather for a ride, then made sure to lock the door behind them as they left.

"Tomorrow's a new day," Henry said. "Maybe tomorrow we'll find the answers to some of these questions."

"I hope so," Jessie said.

* * * *

The next morning, the Aldens got up early and rode their bikes over to Jeff's shop. They were relieved that the gray station wagon didn't seem to be anywhere in sight.

As the Aldens turned onto Jeff's street, they noticed a white sedan parked in front of Mrs. Thorton's house. As the children got closer, they saw a tall man with a black jacket and baseball cap hurry out of the Thorton's house. He quickly got into the white car and started it up.

"Do you suppose that's Erik Thorton?" Violet asked as the white car sped away.

"I don't know who else he could be," Jessie said. "He came out of Mrs. Thorton's house."

"He sure was in a hurry," Benny said.

"I wonder where he's going in such a hurry?" Henry said.

"I don't know," Violet said. "But he was driving a white sedan, not a gray station wagon. So he's probably not the person who was following us."

"Unless the white car is his mother's car and his car is in that garage over there." Jessie pointed to a small one-car garage that sat behind the yellow house.

"That's possible," Henry admitted.

Just then, the children heard sirens. They turned and saw a police car barreling down the middle of the street with lights flashing and sirens blaring.

"Hey, that police car is turning into Jeff's shop!" Jessie cried.

"Come on," Henry said, getting back on his bike. "Let's go see what's going on."

The children pedaled the rest of the way to Jeff's shop. They parked their bikes next to the "Jeff's Custom Furniture" sign, then rushed to the door.

Once inside, they found Jeff and Emily talking to a police officer. The other officer was looking around the shop.

"What's going on here?" Jessie asked. "Why are the police here?"

"It appears someone broke into this shop and vandalized Mr. Naylor's yo-yo last night," a female officer said.

The Aldens turned toward the yo-yo. It was covered in a brown liquid.

"What is it?" Henry asked.

"Looks like oil," another officer replied as he wiped a finger across the liquid.

Jessie gasped. "Who would come in here and pour oil all over the yo-yo?"

"And why?" Violet asked. "Why would someone do such a thing?"

"That's what we're trying to figure out," Emily said coldly. "I was just telling Jeff that you kids were still here when I left last night. I don't know if you are the ones who did this or if you just left the door un-locked—"

"What!" Benny exclaimed.

"You think we're responsible for this?" Violet asked.

"Now, wait a minute," Jeff said. "These kids have been helping me build this yo-yo. I know they're not involved."

The policewoman turned toward the children. The name on her badge was Maguire. "Were you the last ones to leave the shop?"

"Yes," Henry said.

Officer Maguire turned to a new page in her notebook. "And approximately what time was that?"

The children all looked at each other. "Probably around 4:30," Henry said. The others nodded.

"What were you doing here all by yourselves?" Officer Maguire asked.

"We came back over here after we'd been to the library because we wanted to talk to Jeff," Jessie explained. "That was at about four o'clock. He wasn't here, but Emily was. And so was her boyfriend."

Officer Maguire turned back to Emily.

"You didn't mention any boyfriend."

"I-I didn't think that was important," Emily stammered. "But yes, my boyfriend, Todd was with me. He waited while I wrote my letter of resignation. Then, while I was printing it, these kids showed up. I don't know why they came back. They'd been here all morning."

"We wanted to talk to Jeff," Jessie said again. She turned to Jeff. "Did you know that Erik Thorton attempted to build the world's largest yo-yo?"

"But he wasn't successful," Henry added. "When he tried to launch it, it fell off the crane and rolled into the crowd where it injured some people, including Erik."

Emily frowned. "What are you kids talking about?"

"This is why we came back yesterday afternoon," Henry explained. "We wanted to talk to Jeff about all of this."

Officer Maguire kept writing in her notebook. "So, who's Erik Thorton?" she asked, as she wrote.

"He's the son of the lady who lives in that

yellow house across the street. He's here visiting his mother right now. I don't know how he feels, but I'm afraid his mother is not very happy I'm building this yo-yo."

"If her son was injured while attempting to launch the world's largest yo-yo, I'm not surprised to hear that," Officer Maguire said as the other officer joined them.

"Has she or her son made any threats?" the tall officer asked. His badge read: *Sloan*.

"Well," Jeff said slowly. "She did tell me she'd do anything she could to stop me."

"Did you tell the police about that phone call yesterday morning?" Jessie asked Jeff.

"What phone call?" Officer Maguire asked.

"Oh yes. I almost forgot about that," Jeff said. "Jessie, you're the one who answered the phone. Why don't you tell them about it."

So Jessie did, and Officer Maguire copied down everything Jessie said in her note-book.

"Is there anything else we should know about?" Officer Sloan asked.

"Someone's been following us," Benny piped up. "Someone in a gray station wagon."

"Do either of you know anything about this?" Officer Sloan asked Jeff and Emily.

"No," Emily said.

"The kids mentioned something about this yesterday morning," Jeff said.

"We saw the car again when we were having lunch downtown," Violet said.

"And then while we were at the library, somebody took my backpack," Henry added. "I got it back, but I'm afraid whoever took it stole your plans for the yo-yo. I'm really sorry. I should have been more careful."

Jeff's jaw tightened. "Fortunately, I have other copies. But I'm concerned about you kids. You said someone was following you. I had no idea it was this serious."

"I don't think they're following us anymore," Jessie said. "I think they got what they wanted—the plans for your yo-yo. And now someone has broken in here and damaged the yo-yo."

"Can the damage be cleaned up?" Violet asked.

"I don't know," Jeff replied. "But I'm starting to think I should forget about building the world's largest yo-yo. I don't want any trouble."

"Oh, don't do that!" Jessie begged.

"We'll get to the bottom of this," Officer Maguire promised as she closed her notebook.

"That's right," Officer Sloan agreed. "And I think we'll start by paying a visit to your neighbor across the street."

CHAPTER 7

Pizza!

"Do you mind if we come with you when you talk to Mrs. Thorton?" Henry asked the police officers.

"Not at all," Officer Maguire said. "Come on."

So the children followed Officer Sloan and Officer Maguire across the street.

Officer Maguire knocked on Mrs. Thorton's door.

She opened it almost immediately. She looked surprised to see the police officers. "What's this all about?" she asked.

Officer Sloan told Mrs. Thorton that someone had broken into Jeff's shop and poured oil all over it. "Would you know anything about that?" he asked.

Mrs. Thorton drew in her breath. "No, I certainly wouldn't know anything about that."

"It happened early this morning," Officer Maguire said, holding her pen to her notebook. "Did you see anyone suspicious hanging around?"

"No," Mrs. Thorton replied. "But then again, I hardly have time to just stare out the window all day." She let out a short laugh.

"Are you here alone, Mrs. Thorton?" Officer Sloan asked.

"Yes. My son Erik is visiting from New York, but he left a little while ago to look at a house for sale. His company is transferring him back to the Connecticut office, so as soon as he finds a place to live, he's moving back here." Mrs. Thorton smiled.

"Well, I'm sure that makes you happy," Officer Sloan smiled back. "What time did he leave this morning?"

Mrs. Thorton checked her watch. "Oh, about twenty minutes ago. He was running late."

"Can you tell us what kind of car he drives?" Officer Maguire asked.

"He drives a white sedan. Why?" Mrs. Thorton frowned. "Y-you don't think he had anything to do with the trouble across the street, do you?" She looked from one officer to the other with concern.

"We're just gathering facts, Ma'am," Officer Sloan said.

"Then you probably already know that Erik tried to build an over-sized yo-yo, too," Mrs. Thorton said. "And you also know what happened when he tried to launch it."

The officers didn't say anything in response. They just let Mrs. Thorton talk.

"Erik and I are very concerned about this yo-yo that Mr. Naylor is building, and I can assure you that if there's been some trouble over there, neither one of us had anything to do with it!"

The officers thanked Mrs. Thorton for her time, then headed back across the street to Jeff's shop.

Jeff and Emily were mopping up the oil as best they could, but it looked like a lot of the boards on the yo-yo would have to be replaced.

Officer Sloan turned to the children. "Are you kids sure you locked the door when you left the shop last night?"

"Positive," Jessie replied.

"Well, there were no signs of a forced entry," Officer Sloan said. "I think whoever broke in here must have had a key."

"Who all has a key to this place, Mr. Naylor?" Officer Maquire asked.

"Just me and Emily," Jeff said. Then he scowled. "Actually, my former partner, Gary Richmond may still have one, too. We had a falling out . . . I don't think he'd do something like this, but you never know."

Officer Maguire shrugged. "Doesn't hurt to check him out."

Emily glared at the children. "I still think these kids had something to do with it," she said. "Maybe you should check them out a little more, too."

"Now Emily." Jeff held up his hand. "We've talked about this already. I'm sure the Aldens are not to blame."

"Don't be too sure about that," Emily said.

****

On Monday, Jeff called the Aldens on the phone and invited them to go out for lunch. "I know you kids aren't responsible for the damage to the yo-yo," he explained. "And I'd like to prove it by taking you and your grandfather out for a nice lunch at the Leaning Tower of Pizza. Do you like pizza?"

"Yes, but you don't have to take us out for lunch," Jessie said.

"I know I don't have to," Jeff said. "But I want to. Are you available?"

Grandfather already had lunch plans, but the children were free. So Grandfather dropped them off at the Leaning Tower of Pizza at 11:30.

When the children arrived, Jeff was already there. He waved to them from a back booth.

"Hi, Jeff." Jessie slid into the bench next to Jeff while Henry, Violet, and Benny sat down on the other side of the table that was covered with a red and white checked table cloth.

"Hi, kids. I'm glad you could make it."

Jeff passed the menus around and for the next couple of minutes everyone read them over. They finally settled on two pizzas: a large pepperoni with extra cheese and a medium sausage and mushroom.

A waitress whose name tag said *Adele* came over with a tray full of glasses and a pitcher of soda. Then she took their order. "I'll get those pizzas out to you as soon as I can," she said.

The pizza place was busy, so the Aldens knew there would be a bit of a wait.

"Do the police have any idea who broke into your shop the other night?" Henry asked as he took a sip of his soda.

"I'm afraid not," Jeff replied. "They

talked to Gary, but he didn't know anything about it."

"Have you worked on the yo-yo at all since we were last in your shop?" Violet asked.

"I've cleaned it up some. But at this point, I'm not sure how much of it is really salvageable."

"Still, you're not really going to quit building it, are you?" Benny asked.

"No, I guess not," Jeff admitted. "I started this project, so I'd really like to see it through. I don't know whether I'll get credit for the record. Not unless I find that missing flash card with all the footage from when we first started building."

"You still haven't found that?" Henry asked, surprised.

"No," Jeff said as he stirred his soda. "I've looked everywhere. But I'm not going to worry about it. At this point, I just want to finish the yo-yo. I don't care about the record."

"We'll help you any way we can," Violet promised.

"I appreciate that," Jeff said. "With Emily quitting, I'm going to need all the help I can get."

"You can count on us," Jessie said.

"I'm glad," Jeff said. "I had no idea Emily and her boyfriend were planning on starting a woodworking business. I certainly thought she'd stick around until after the yo-yo was finished. She seemed really interested in that project. I even gave her a copy of the plans."

"You did?" Henry asked.

"Sure. She asked if she could have a copy as a souvenir," Jeff said.

"Do you have anybody else in mind for Emily's job?" Violet asked.

"No. I called the newspaper this morning and told them I wanted to place an ad. The ad will run this weekend. We'll see if I get any calls," Jeff said.

"More soda, please," Benny said, sliding his glass toward the pitcher.

Jessie reached for the pitcher, but something in the corner of her eye caught her attention. "Not again," she said, staring out the window. Her hand still gripped the pitcher.

"What?" asked Henry. He, Benny, and Violet all turned to see what she was looking at.

"That gray station wagon," Jessie said. "I just saw it drive by."

"I sure wish I knew whose car that was," Henry said.

A few minutes later, a tall, skinny man walked into the pizza shop. He was alone. He was wearing a red baseball cap that was turned backwards and chewing on a toothpick.

"Be with you in a minute, sir," Adele said as she rushed past him with two pizzas. She set the piping hot pizzas down in the middle of the Aldens' table.

"Can I get you anything else?" the waitress asked.

"I don't think so," Henry said. He turned to Jeff, but Jeff's eyes were glued to the man standing in the doorway.

The man in the doorway stared back at Jeff. The toothpick in his mouth fell to the floor, but he didn't even notice. He slowly backed up—right into the door. Then he spun around, whipped the door open, and left.

"Sir?" The waitress peered nervously at Jeff. "Are you all right?"

"What?" Jeff turned to the waitress in confusion. "Oh yes. Yes, I'm fine. Thank you."

The waitress left and Jeff slid the pizza closer to Henry. "You kids help yourselves," he said as craned his neck to see out the door.

Henry dished up slices of steaming pizza and put them on all the plates.

"Who was that man, Jeff?" Violet asked.

Jeff was still staring at the door. He turned to Violet. "That was my former partner, Gary Richmond."

A couple minutes later, Jessie noticed the gray station wagon go by again.

"Jeff, does Gary drive a gray station wagon?" Jessie asked.

"Did you see that car again, Jessie?" Henry asked.

"Yes. It just went by again," Jessie replied. "But this time it was going in the opposite direction it was going in before."

Jeff thought for a minute. "Gary used to drive a red pick-up. But it's been so long since we've seen each other that I honestly don't know what he drives now. I have to say, I haven't seen his pick-up around town in quite a while, though. I used to see it all the time. So it's certainly possible he's gotten something else by now."

"Do you think he's the one who's been following us?" Benny asked as he took a bite of his pizza.

"I don't know," Jessie replied. "He didn't act like someone who'd been following us when he came in here. He seemed surprised to see us."

"Or surprised to see me," Jeff said.

He and the Aldens finished their food, then Jeff strolled over to the cash register to pay. When he came back, he told the Aldens, "I'm expecting another load of lumber tomorrow, so maybe you can come back late tomorrow afternoon and we'll see what we can salvage of that yo-yo."

"Sure," Henry said. "We'll be there."

CHAPTER 8

An Old Friend

"I'd sure like to know whether Gary's the one who's been following us," Jessie said.

"And I'd like to find out whether he's the one who took the plans out of my backpack," Henry said. "Remember, he and Jeff were originally going to build the yo-yo together. Maybe Gary heard that Jeff was starting on it by himself and he didn't like that. So maybe he wanted to see whether

Jeff was using the plans they'd made together."

"That would explain why he'd want the plans, all right," Violet said.

"He's probably still got a key to Jeff's shop," Jessie said. "He could've broken into the shop when no one was there and stolen the flash card out of Jeff's camera. That way Jeff wouldn't be able to prove he built the yo-yo and get credit for the record."

"That's a good point," Henry said. "He probably doesn't want Jeff to get credit for building the world's largest yo-yo without him."

"This all sounds very logical," Violet said. "But there's still one problem."

"What's that?" Benny asked.

"We don't know for sure that Gary drives a gray station wagon," Violet said.

"Yes, but we can find out pretty easily," Henry said. "All we have to do is find out where he lives. Then we can go over to his house and see if there's a gray station wagon parked out front or in his garage."

"We could go over to the library and

look up his address in the phone book," Benny suggested.

"Yes, let's do that," Jessie said. "I think it's time we paid Gary a visit."

"If he drives a gray station wagon, he'll have some explaining to do," Henry said.

So the Aldens hurried over to the library.

"I know where the phone books are," Benny said as soon as they stepped inside. "Follow me." He rushed ahead of the others.

Henry, Jessie and Violet followed Benny past the reference desk and over to a low shelf by the windows.

"Ta da!" Benny said, gesturing toward the shelf. It was filled with phone books from all over the United States.

Jessie found the Greenfield, Connecticut phone book on the second shelf. She pulled it out and started rifling through it, looking for Richmond, Gary. The others gathered around her and scanned the pages, too.

"Here it is," Jessie said, running her finger down the list of Richmonds. "Gary Richmond. 2440 Highland Drive."

"That's only a few blocks from here," Henry said.

"Let's go!" Benny said.

Jessie put the phone book back and the Aldens set out for 2440 Highland Drive.

The houses in this part of town were old, two-story homes that had been restored slowly over time. Many did not have garages.

The Aldens walked along Highland Drive until they came to 2440. A white picket fence surrounded the house. Flowers lined the front walk. And a gray station wagon was parked next to the back door.

"Looks like we solved the mystery of who owns the gray station wagon," Henry said.

"Gary Richmond," Violet said.

"But we still don't know whether Gary's really been following us or if it's just been a coincidence that we've seen his car everywhere we've been," Jessie said.

"Well, it looks like he's home," Benny said, opening the white gate that blocked the front walk. "Let's go talk to him."

The Aldens went up the walk, clattered up the wood steps and rang the bell. The

door opened and the Aldens stood face-to-face with the man they'd just seen at the Leaning Tower of Pizza. His mouth opened in surprise when he saw the Aldens standing on his front porch.

"Hello, Mr. Richmond," Jessie said politely. "Do you know who we are?"

"I don't know your names, but I know who you are," Gary said coolly. "You're friends of my former business partner, Jeff Naylor." His right eye twitched when he said Jeff's name.

"That's right," Henry said. "Could we speak with you, Mr. Richmond?"

He hesitated for a few seconds, then opened the door. "Please, call me Gary," he said as he stepped outside.

"Now, what's this all about?" Gary asked.

"We want to know if you've been following us," Benny blurted.

"Benny." Jessie nudged him. That was indeed what they wanted to know, but Jessie wouldn't have asked quite so bluntly.

"That's okay," Gary said. "I can see why you'd think that. We've been ending up in a lot of the same places lately."

"Yes. Why is that?" Henry asked. "Do you know?"

"Well, I didn't know you all were going to be at the Leaning Tower of Pizza today. And I certainly didn't know Jeff Naylor was going to be there," Gary said. "Believe me, if I had known, I never would've gone in there."

"What about all the other times?" Jessie asked. "Did you mean to follow us home from Jeff's shop the other night? Did you follow us to the library?"

"Did you take some papers out of my backpack?" Henry asked.

Gary let out a breath of air, then slumped back against the doorframe. "Yes, I did," he admitted. "But it's not what you think. I helped design those plans. They were half mine!"

"We know you helped design them," Violet said.

"You do?" Gary asked. "How do you know that?"

"Jeff told us," Benny said. "He said you

and he were going to build the yo-yo together."

"That's what we'd always planned," Gary
said, rubbing his forehead. "But then we
had that falling out a few months ago. I
thought the yo-yo was as finished as our
friendship. We certainly can't build a yo-yo
together if we're not speaking, can we?"

Violet bit her tongue. She wanted to ask
Gary why he didn't just make up with Jeff,
but she didn't want to interrupt Gary.

"About a week ago, I heard people talking in town," Gary went on. "They said Jeff
was working on something really amazing.
They said he was building the world's
largest yo-yo."

"Well, Jeff never told me he was contin-
uing with the project," Gary said. "So I had
to see it for myself. I snuck into the shop
one night after he and that woman he's
got working for him left. I still had a key
from when I worked there. I saw the
yo-yo. Or, I saw the start of it, anyway.
It was just like we'd planned.

"What I really wanted was to get my

hands on the plans for the yo-yo. I tried booting up Jeff's computer. I figured he had to have the plans on there somewhere. But he'd changed his password since I worked with him. I couldn't get into the computer. I came back the next night, thinking I'd search the shop once everybody went home. But then I saw Jeff come out and give the plans to you. That's why I started following you. I thought it would be easier to get the plans from you than it would be to find another copy in Jeff's shop."

"So you did follow us to the library and you did take them out of my backpack," Henry said.

Gary looked down at the ground. "Yes," he admitted. "But I just wanted to see whether he was using the plans we'd made together or whether he'd come up with a whole new set of plans."

That was exactly what the Aldens had suspected.

"Did you take Jeff's flash card out of his camera, too?" Jessie asked.

Gary's eyebrows scrunched together.

"Flash card? What's a flash card?"

"You don't know what a flash card is?" Benny asked, surprised.

"No."

"It's a little card that's used to store data," Henry explained. "Jeff had a flash card in his digital video camera. He said he needed to record all the steps in building the yo-yo if he wanted to get credit for breaking the record."

"That's right," Gary nodded. "You have to prove you really broke the record. Are you saying Jeff had a recording of what he'd done so far, but the recording is now missing?"

"Yes," Violet said.

Gary scratched his neck. "I admit I took the plans, but I didn't take anything out of his camera. And I didn't vandalize the yo-yo, either. I wouldn't do something like that. I was hurt that Gary ever even thought I would. The police came to talk to me, you know."

"Yes, we know," Henry said. "But they said there was no forced entry that night, so they wanted to talk to everyone who had a key to Jeff's shop."

"Jeff told the police that even though you'd had a falling out, he didn't think you'd really come in and damage the yo-yo like that."

"He did?" Gary seemed surprised.

"Yes," the children answered in unison.

"What did you think of Jeff's plans for the yo-yo?" Henry asked. "Were they pretty similar to what you two had planned together?"

"Yes and no," Gary replied. "It looks to me as though he used our original plans to start with, but he's also made some modifications." Gary walked over to a small writing desk across the room. He opened the top drawer and brought out some papers. The plans for the yo-yo!

He came back and spread them out on the coffee table in front of the children. "See here?" he pointed at one of the sketches of a yo-yo half. "It was my idea to build it in layers like this. I told Jeff that was the only way to keep the yo-yo light enough for us for us manage."

Gary pointed to one of the other draw-ings. "But these layers here are different. I don't know why Jeff would build the thir-teenth and fourteenth layers like this."

"Is there something wrong with the way he's doing it?" Violet asked.

"Is it unsafe?" Benny asked.

"Well, his way is going to make the yo-yo heavier," Gary said as he sat back down. "He's using some of the strongest cable available for the string, so it should still be fine. But I don't know why he wouldn't want to build the yo-yo as light as possible. Lighter is always better."

"Have you asked Jeff why he is doing it this way?" Violet asked.

"Oh no," Gary shook his head. "Like I said, we had a falling out. We haven't spoken in more than six months."

"Would you like to speak again?" Benny asked. "Would you like to make up?"

Gary sighed. "Sure, I'd like to. But I don't think Jeff wants that."

"How do you know?" Violet asked.

"Have you asked him?"

"Well, no. But . . ." Jeff's voice trailed off.

"But what?" Henry asked.

Gary shrugged. He didn't say anything more.

The Aldens all glanced at one another. Jeff always seemed a little sad when he talked about Gary. And now Gary had come right out and said he'd like to make up with Jeff. There had to be a way to get the two of them together.

"Did you know that Emily, the woman you saw at Jeff's shop, is quitting?" Jessie asked suddenly.

"No, I didn't," Gary said.

"I wonder what would happen if you went to Jeff and asked for your old job back?" Jessie asked.

"Oh, I couldn't do that," Gary said right away.

"Why not?" the children asked.

At first Gary didn't say anything. He just looked from one Alden to the next. "Do you all think I should go over there and talk to Jeff?"

"Yes. Of course. Absolutely," the Aldens responded.

"You don't think he'll tell me to go away?" Gary looked worried.

"Well, there's only one way to find out," Jessie said. "You're already not speaking to each other," Henry pointed out. "So if he does send you away, you won't be any worse off than you are now."

"But I don't think he'll send you away," Violet said.

"You're right," Gary said, slapping his legs and rising to his feet. "Let's go."

CHAPTER 9

Making Up

Jeff's eyes narrowed when he saw Gary. "What are you doing here?"

"He came here to make up with you, Jeff," Violet said right away.

"He wants his old job back," Benny put in.

Jeff glanced curiously over at Gary. His expression softened. "Is that true?"

"Maybe," Gary said carefully. "We have some things to work out first."

Jeff nodded. "I'd like to do that. I've known you my whole life, Gary. So many

104

times I've wanted to just pick up the phone and call you."

"Me, too," Gary said as the two of them walked over to a corner to talk.

"Do you think they'll make up?" Violet asked.

"I think so," Jessie said. "They're talking, aren't they?"

"Should we wait for them to finish or should we just go home?" Henry asked.

"I don't want to interrupt them," Jessie said. "And I don't want to leave without saying goodbye. So let's wait."

"I'm glad Gary isn't the one who damaged the yo-yo," Violet said.

"I'm glad, too," Benny said. "But if it wasn't him, who was it?"

"It had to be someone who had a key to this shop," Henry said. "But the only other person besides Jeff and Gary who has a key is Emily."

"But why would Emily vandalize the yo-yo?" Jessie asked. "She's helped work on it."

"Maybe it wasn't Emily. Maybe it was her boyfriend." Benny suggested.

"Maybe," Jessie agreed. "But why would he vandalize it?"

"I don't know," Violet said with a sigh. "It's a mystery, all right."

Everyone seemed to be lost in their own thoughts, so Benny took out his yo-yo to help pass the time.

"Hey, have you learned how to throw a sleeper yet, Benny?" Violet asked.

"Not yet," Benny said. "But I have learned another trick. Watch this. This is called monkey on a string."

Benny let out the string on the yo-yo, then held the string by left index finger so the yo-yo hung about three inches below his finger. He threaded the string into the side of the yo-yo, then pulled down with his right hand so the yo-yo moved up the string. When it got to the top, Benny slipped his left finger out and the yo-yo went back down to his right hand.

"Wow," Jessie said.

Violet clapped her hands. "That was awesome, Benny!"

"Thanks," Benny said. "But I still wish

I could do a sleeper. Once I learn that, there are tons of other tricks I'll be able to do."

"You'll get it," Henry said. "If you just—"

"*Keep practicing*," Benny said along with Henry.

The others laughed.

"That's what everybody always says," Benny said. "But I've been practicing a lot. And I just can't get it."

Benny tried to practice his sleeper some more. He tried flicking his wrist the way Grandfather showed him, but it just didn't work. Still, one way or another, Benny was determined to learn that trick.

"Hey, look!" Violet pointed. "Jeff and Gary are over by the yo-yo."

It looked like their conversation was over. And it looked like they'd made up.

"I think we can still salvage some of this," Gary was telling Jeff. "Most of the mess is confined to the top two layers here. If we pull those boards off, we can probably wipe up what's spilled inside."

Jeff walked slowly around the yo-yo, surveying the damage.

"Then all we have to do is rebuild these two layers," Gary went on. "It shouldn't take that long if we work together. And I'll bet these kids would be willing to help." He glanced up at the Aldens.

"Oh yes," Jessie said eagerly. "We sure would."

"I suppose it's worth a try," Jeff said.

He grabbed his electric screwdriver and started loosening the screws on one side of the yo-yo. Gary grabbed another screwdriver and started loosening screws on the other side of the yo-yo.

"Maybe you kids should grab some safety goggles," Jeff said as he pulled out one of the damaged boards and tossed it in a barrel.

The children looked around. There were three pairs of safety goggles on the shelf above the coat rack, but they needed four.

"I see Emily's work jacket hanging on a hook over there." Jeff pointed. "Why don't you check her pockets. Maybe she's got some safety goggles in there?"

Jessie, Violet and Benny put on the safety goggles that they'd found. Henry reached inside Emily's work jacket. There was indeed a pair of safety goggles in there. But there was also something else.

A tiny flash card. It was labeled simply "yo-yo."

* * * *

Jeff frowned. Then he picked up the phone and called Emily at home. "Could you please come down to the shop right now?" he asked. "Yes, I know today is your day off, but this is very important. There are some things I need to ask you and I want to ask them in person."

Jeff listened for a few seconds then said, "Thank you, Emily. I'll see you in half an hour."

"I can't believe Emily took the flash card," Violet said. "She seemed so nice."

"She *is* nice," Jeff said. "I'll be curious to hear what she has to say for herself."

While they waited for Emily to arrive, the group continued to pull apart the damaged pieces of the yo-yo.

"See?" Gary said when they got a few layers lower into the yo-yo. "The rest of these pieces look fine."

"I guess you're right," Jeff said.

The door opened and Emily walked in. She hung back by the door. "Y-you wanted me to stop by, Jeff?" she said nervously.

"Yes." Jeff motioned for her to come closer. "I want to show you something."

Emily moved as though her legs were pulling heavy weights.

"We needed an extra pair of safety goggles," Jeff began. "So I told the children to check the pockets of your work jacket. They found my flash card in your pocket." He reached into his own pocket and pulled out the flash card.

Emily looked down at the floor.

"Did you vandalize the yo-yo, too?" Jeff asked.

Emily sighed. "Todd and I did it together. I also canceled the order of the

wood. I knew you needed that wood, but I canceled it anyway. And Todd was the one who called and warned you to stop building the yo-yo."

"Why, Emily?" Jessie asked. "Why would you and Todd do these things?"

Emily sat down on a metal stool. "It's hard to explain. Todd and I have been nervous about all the attention you've been getting for this yo-yo. We were afraid with all the attention on you, it would be hard for us to make a name for ourselves with our own custom furniture shop. Everybody will want to keep going to the guy who built the giant yo-yo."

"It takes time to build a reputation, Emily," Gary said. "Surely you and Todd must realize that?"

"Yes, we do. Especially in this community where everyone already knows and respects Jeff," Emily said. "But we started thinking that if for some reason you didn't get the yo-yo built, then maybe we could build it. That's why I asked you for a copy of your plans. Todd and I were hoping if we were the ones who built the world's largest yo-yo, then people would want to hire us to build things for them instead of you. I'm really sorry, Jeff. You've been so nice to me these past two months and I've really learned a lot about the woodworking business. We should never have tried to stop you from building this yo-yo."

"Well, my friend here thinks that some of our work can be salvaged," Jeff said, nodding toward Gary. "We're not going to have to start over."

"I'm glad to hear that," Emily said. "In fact, I've been rethinking my resignation. I'm not sure I want to go into business with Todd anymore. Maybe I should stay here and keep working with you, Jeff? That is, if you'll still have me after what I've done."

Jeff and Gary exchanged glances. "Well, I might've been inclined to give you another chance, Emily, but my old friend Gary has decided to come back to work," Jeff said with a smile. He patted his old friend on the back. "So I'm afraid that job is no longer available."

Emily shrugged. "I guess I can't blame you for that," she said. "But on the bright side, I'm glad the two of you are friends again. Whenever Jeff talked about you, Gary, I could tell how much he missed you."

"You missed me?" Gary asked.

"Of course I missed you," Jeff replied.

Gary smiled. "I missed you, too, old friend."

CHAPTER 10

The Launch

The next day, Karl's Lumber delivered another of load of boards. The Aldens helped Jeff and Gary with the yo-yo every day. They cut and measured each piece of wood, then pounded them all together. When they finished, they had two yo-yo halves. They coated each half with a drywall compound, then it was time to paint.

"Hmm. I don't know what color we

should paint the yo-yo," Jeff said.

"How about purple?" Violet suggested. Purple was her favorite color.

"Purple is a great color for a yo-yo," Gary said.

So they painted each half purple.

Then, all they needed to do was attach the two sides of the yo-yo to the axle and wind the rope. They brought Gary's truck into the shop to help lift the pieces up on to their sides so they could be put together.

"Are you sure this cable is going to be strong enough?" Benny asked when Jeff attached the rope to the axle.

"It should be," Gary said. "Come and look how thick it is."

Benny could hardly stretch his hand around the rope. "Wow! That's thick!" Benny said.

The Aldens watched as Jeff and Gary cranked the rope to the yo-yo. When they finished, they all stepped back to admire their work.

"It looks just like a real yo-yo!" Violet said. "Now all we have to do is see if it works like a real yo-yo," Gary said.

They called the A-1 Wrecking Company to come and pick up the yo-yo and take it to North Ridge Park, which was where the launch was scheduled to occur.

"How are we going to get the yo-yo outside?" Jessie asked.

"We'll have to roll it," Jeff said. He opened the big garage door at the front of the shop.

"Will it go through the door?" Violet wondered.

"It should," Jeff replied. "The yo-yo is twelve feet tall and the door is twelve and a half feet tall."

By the time they rolled the yo-yo all the way outside, the truck from A-1 Wrecking had arrived. A man hopped down from the cab of the truck to help.

"Hey, that's some yo-yo," the man said, glancing at the yo-yo in fascination. "Will it really work?"

"We'll find out tomorrow," Gary said.

The man from A-1 put a ramp up against the back of the truck. Then he attached the rope from the yo-yo to the crane and slowly pulled the yo-yo up onto the truck.

Across the street, both Mrs. Thorton and her son Erik stood under the tall maple tree in their front yard and watched. The Aldens walked across the street.

"We haven't actually met," Henry said to Erik. "But we're the Aldens. We're friends of Jeff Naylor's."

"You're the kids who have been helping Jeff with his yo-yo," Erik said as he shook hands with the children.

"Yes," Jessie said. "We read all about the yo-yo you built a few years ago. We're sorry it didn't work."

"So am I," Erik said. "But maybe this one will work. I'm sure you all have worked very hard."

"We have," Benny said.

"Are you going to come to the launch tomorrow?" Violet asked.

"I'm planning on it," Erik said.

"I'll be there, too," Mrs. Thorton said. "But I'll be standing in the back, just in case there's any trouble."

"That's fine," Jessie said. "I'm just glad you'll be there."

* * * *

The Aldens couldn't have asked for a more perfect Saturday morning. It was sunny and warm. Not a cloud could be seen across the bright blue sky.

It was only eight o'clock, but already people had started to gather in North Ridge Park. The yo-yo hung from the top of a two hundred-foot crane in the middle of the park. A wide area around the yo-yo had been roped off for safety reasons. And the paramedics were on hand, just in case they were needed.

The launch was scheduled for nine o'clock.

"Are you nervous?" Grandfather asked Jeff as the Aldens stood around with Jeff and Gary.

"A little," Jeff admitted. "Mostly I'm just excited. This project has been in the works for a long time."

Finally, at nine A.M., the mayor stepped forward with a microphone and welcomed everyone to this historic event. Then he turned the microphone over to Jeff. Henry recorded everything with Jeff's digital video camera. Jeff introduced himself and Gary, then told a little about the yo-yo and how they'd come to build it.

"Does it really work?" somebody in the crowd called out.

"Let's find out," Jeff said. He turned to the man from A-1 Wrecking, who was operating the crane, to see if he was ready. When he nodded that he was, Jeff began a countdown.

"Ten . . . nine . . . eight . . . seven, six, five, four, three, two, one—"

All eyes were fixed on the yo-yo. There wasn't a sound in North Ridge Park.

Then the yo-yo was released. There was a collective gasp from the crowd as the yo-yo started down the cable. What would happen when it reached the bottom? Would it fall from the crane and crash to the ground? Would it just stay there at the bottom? Or would it start back up again?

The Aldens hardly dared to breathe as the yo-yo got closer to the bottom of the rope. When it reached the bottom, it started back up again.

The crowd cheered. Jeff and Gary hugged. Erik Thorton and his mother smiled. The Aldens jumped up and down.

The yo-yo yo-ed eight times before coming to a rest at the bottom of the cable. It had worked! Jeff, Gary, and the Aldens had indeed built the world's largest yo-yo.

* * * *

A couple weeks later, the Aldens were visiting Jeff and Gary in their shop.

"Look at this, everyone," Jeff said, waving a letter in the air. "Our yo-yo is going to be in next year's record book. "Hooray!" Everyone cheered.

"I just want to thank you kids for being part of this," Jeff said. "And thank you for bringing Gary and me together again."

The Aldens smiled. "Thank you for letting us be part of it," Henry said.

"We're glad you and Gary are friends again," Benny said as he took out his yo-yo and tried to throw a sleeper. This time, when the yo-yo reached the bottom of the string, it kept spinning.

Benny stared wide-eyed at the yo-yo. "Hey!" he said. "Look at that! I'm doing it! I'm really doing it!"

"You certainly are," Gary said.

"Now see if you can pull it back up," Jeff said.

Benny raised his hand and the yo-yo climbed back up the string to his hand.

"I can't believe it!" Benny said. He immediately tossed the yo-yo down again. And once again, the yo-yo spun a perfect sleeper.

Benny lowered the yo-yo to the ground and let it walk-the-dog for a couple of feet, then pulled it back up.

"I knew you'd get it, Benny," Violet said.

"So now I can do a sleeper, walk-the-dog, and monkey-on-a-string. I wonder what other tricks I can do," Benny said.

"I have a feeling you can do anything you set your mind to, Benny," Jeff said.

Benny grinned. "All it takes is a little practice."

GERTRUDE CHANDLER WARNER discovered when she was teaching that many readers who like an exciting story could find no books that were both easy and fun to read. She decided to try to meet this need, and her first book, *The Boxcar Children*, quickly proved she had succeeded.

Miss Warner drew on her own experiences to write the mystery. As a child she spent hours watching trains go by on the tracks opposite her family home. She often dreamed about what it would be like to set up housekeeping in a caboose or freight car— the situation the Alden children find themselves in.

While the mystery element is central to each of Miss Warner's books, she never thought of them as strictly juvenile mysteries. She liked to stress the Aldens' independence and resourcefulness and their solid New England devotion to using up and making do. The Aldens go about most of their adventures with as little adult supervision as possible—something else that delights young readers.

Miss Warner lived in Putnam, Connecticut, until her death in 1979. During her lifetime, she received hundreds of letters from girls and boys telling her how much they liked her books.